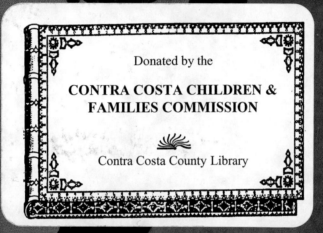

Published by Roaring Brook Press, A division of The Millbrook Press,
2 Old New Milford Road, Brookfield, Connecticut 06804
All rights reserved Library of Congress Cataloging-in-Publication Data Hru, Dakari, 1952-
Tickle, Tickle / by Dakari Hru ; pictures by Ken Wilson-Max. p. cm.

Summary: A baby boy who has lots of fun when his father plays with him.
[1. Fathers and sons – Fiction. 2. Babies – Fiction. 3. Stories in rhyme.] Wilson–Max, Ken, ill. II.Title.
PZ8.3H844 Ti 2002 [E]–dc22001041715

ISBN 0 – 7613 – 2468 – 2 (library binding)
10 9 8 7 6 5 4 3 2 1

ISBN 0 – 7613 – 1537 – 3 (trade)
10 9 8 7 6 5 4 3 2 1
Printed in Hong Kong/China

First edition

written by **Dakari Hru**

Tickle
Tickle

illustrated by **Ken Wilson-Max**

ROARING BROOK PRESS

me papa tickle me feet

he call it "finger treat"

me scream and run each time he come

me papa tickle me feet

he tickle me tummy, me chest, me arm
his fingers fly so wild

he say, "Come here, little man.

You my ticklin' chile."

me papa say he love me
me papa look so proud

he say, "Sonny, what a joy

to see you laugh out loud."

he tickle me ribs, me neck, me back

his fingers grow longer each day

me twist and swing and laugh and kick
but he hold me anyway

me eyes, they water
me throat be sore
me weak, me dizzy
but me want more

he throw me high up in the air
and catch me from behind

me say, "Go higher!" and he say,
"Don't you know you're mine?"

me papa tickle me feet
he call it "finger treat"

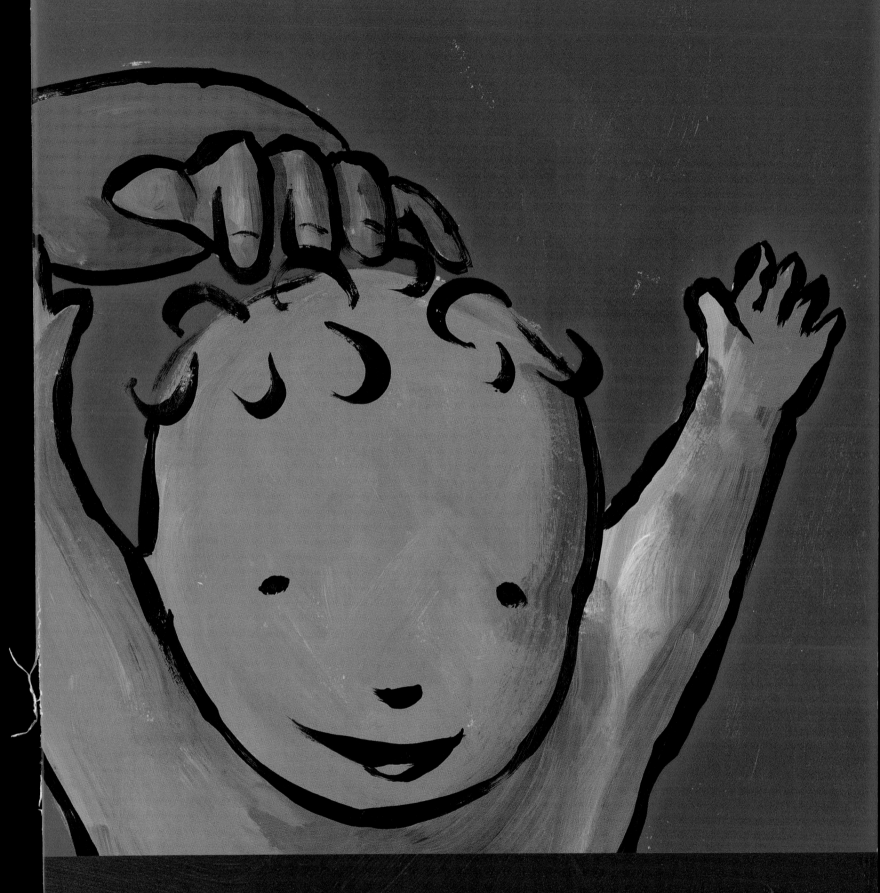

me scream and run (but OH, WHAT FUN!)

when papa tickle me feet.